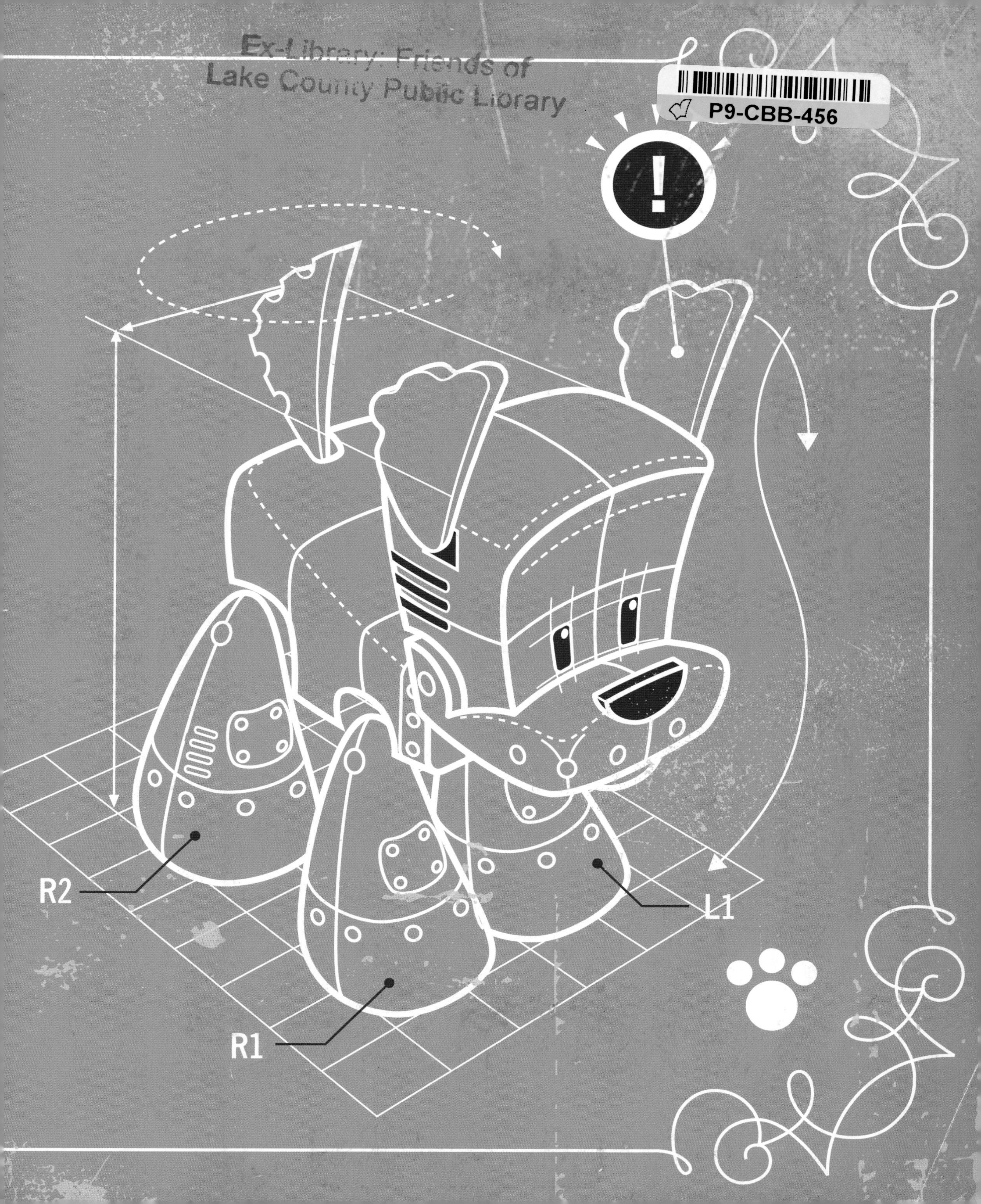
R2
R1
L1

To my very own
"Scrap," Lorcan
—MO

International Standard Book Number: 1-56148-489-X

Library of Congress Catalog Card Number: 2005002669

Original edition published in English by Little Tiger Press,
an imprint of Magi Publications, London, England, 2005.

Printed in China

Library of Congress Cataloging-in-Publication Data

Oliver, Mark, 1960-
Robot dog / Mark Oliver.
p. cm.

Summary: In the junkyard where they live, Scrap and the other
slightly defective robot dogs find a surprising new owner.
ISBN 1-56148-489-X (hardcover)
[1. Dogs--Fiction. 2. Automata--Fiction.] I. Title.

PZ7.O482Rob 2005
[E]--dc22
2005002669

ROBOT DOG

MARK OLIVER

Good Books
Intercourse, PA 17534

In a factory, on a hill,
a huge machine made
robot dogs.

D #2302
D #2301

The robot dogs rolled out of the factory and were delivered to owners who played with them and loved them and cared for them.

The dogs were very happy because all dogs, even robot dogs, want an owner.

One little dog on the conveyor belt was very excited.

"I wonder what my owner will be like," he said. "What will I be called?"

He was much too excited to sit still — he jumped and frolicked and bounced up and down. But then,

CRASH!

He bounced too high and clonked his ear. At once alarm bells rang, red lights flashed and a cloud of smoke whooshed as the huge machine ground slowly to a stop.

2304

The machine inspected the robot dog very carefully. Finally a voice boomed:

"NOT RUSTY OR DUSTY,
NOT BATTERED OR BENT,
NO PATCHES OR SCRATCHES,
BUT THERE IS A DENT!

SCRAP!"

"So that's my name!" thought Scrap as the machine picked him up and dropped him through a hatch.

Whhhheeeeeee!

Scrap slid down a chute
and landed in a yard full of junk.
There, staring at him, were
some other dogs.
"Hello!" he said. "I'm Scrap!
Where am I? Where's my owner?"
One of the dogs said, "You don't have
an owner — you're a reject like us."

mum

Bumper, Dent, Scratch and Sniffer all lived in the yard. They made it comfortable, and it was a wonderful place to play, just a bit messy, the way dogs like it.

They often played with other dogs who had owners. But sooner or later their owners would call:

"Come on, Shiny."
"Dinner time, Sparkle."

Then they stopped whatever they were doing and ran home.

Seeing the other dogs go off happily to their owners made the yard dogs feel a bit sad.

"Why don't we get an owner?"
said Scrap one day.

"They take a lot of looking after," replied Bumper. "They like things to be tidy, and you need to play games and fuss over them to keep them happy."

But the more they all talked about it, the more they *really* wanted an owner.

"How can we get one?" said Sniffer. "We're rejects!"

"There must be a way," thought Scrap.

As Scrap started thinking, the cogs in his brain started turning. They went around faster and faster as he thought harder and harder.

Finally a light flickered on!

"I've got an idea!" Scrap announced to the other dogs, excitedly. "Come and help me!"

The dogs raced around collecting anything that might be useful.

They worked all day and all night, and by the next morning the dogs were exhausted, but very proud, because . . .

. . . there stood an owner!

He was rusty and dusty, battered and bent, patched, scratched and covered in dents — but he had a heart of gold.

2

Their owner played with
them and loved them and
cared for them. And the dogs
were very happy, because all
dogs, even robot dogs,
want an owner.

#0000